For Zachary, Shaw, and Caroline,
for whom Christmas is never lost.

R.C.B.

1 2 3 4 5 6 7 8 9 10   16 15 14 13 12 11 10 09 08 07

What Happened to Merry Christmas?

By Robert C. Baker ★ Art by Dave Hill

CONCORDIA PUBLISHING HOUSE · SAINT LOUIS

In a town very much like your town and on a street very much like your street, lived a boy named Sam. And Sam was in a hurry.

"Merry Christmas is lost!" Sam shouted as he leaped off the school bus and onto his driveway. Sam dashed across the front lawn, threw open the front door, ran right through the living room, and burst into the kitchen.

In his fist was a piece of paper.

"What's wrong, Sam?" Mother called from her office in the next room.

"Merry Christmas is lost!" Sam, now quite out of breath, tried to shout again as he collapsed into a chair.

Mother rushed into the kitchen. Laying her hand upon Sam's shoulder, she asked, "Tell me, what is lost?"

"Merry Christmas!" Sam whispered.

"But how can that be?" Mother asked.

"Here," Sam said, handing her the piece of paper. It was an invitation. Sam had been invited to a party in December, but it wasn't a Christmas party. It was a *holiday* party.

"Teacher says there won't be any Christmas," Sam said, tears welling in his eyes.

"The holiday party sounds like it will be a lot of fun," Mother said. "Your school friends will be there, and the invitation says there will be cookies and presents."

"But what about *Christmas?*" Sam wanted to know.

His mother thought for a moment. Then she said, "Maybe Christmas really *isn't* lost, Sam. Just because something is not easy to *find* does not mean it is *lost*. Maybe we will just have to look a little harder for it."

Mother was always good about explaining things so Sam could understand.

"Where?" Sam asked. "Where do we look for Christmas?"

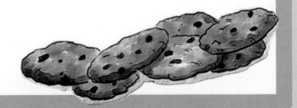

"Well, first," Mother said as she pointed to the window, "see the snowflake you made in school?"

"Yes," Sam said. His snowflake was taped to the glass.

"You made a beautiful snowflake, Sam. However, who makes all the snowflakes, the real ones that fall from the sky in the winter?"

"God does," Sam answered.

"Yes, He does. And how many sides does this snowflake have?" she continued.

"Each snowflake has six sides." Sam knew the answer because on the day they made snowflakes they had also talked about the number six.

"That's right. Each snowflake has six sides, and each snowflake is special because it is different from all the others. Snowflakes remind us that God created the world in six days. On the sixth day, God made people. He said, **"Let us make man in Our image"** (Genesis 1:26). Since that time each and every boy and girl have been special. You are very special to me and to Dad, to God and to Jesus."

"Sam," Mother continued, "now look over here." His mother had walked from the kitchen to the dining room with Sam right behind. "What do you see on the table?" she asked.

"A wreath with some candles," Sam replied.

"That's right," Sam's mother said. "This is an Advent wreath. It reminds us that Christmas is coming. Each Sunday in December we light a candle. By Christmas all four will be lit. The candles remind us that Jesus is "the light of the world" (John 8:12). He came to take away the darkness of our sins by dying on the cross."

"What about the Christmas tree?" Sam asked.

"Well," Mother replied, "evergreen trees are used for Christmas trees. Evergreens are always green; they are always alive. What do we celebrate at Christmas?"

"Jesus' birthday!" Sam shouted.

"Right. And when do we celebrate Jesus being alive again?" she asked.

"Easter!" Sam said.

"Exactly. On the first Easter, the angels told the women that Jesus was not in the grave. They said, 'He is not here, but has risen'" (Luke 24:6).

"And what about the angels?" Sam wondered. "The ones on the tree."

"The angel at top of the tree can remind us of the angel Gabriel, who told Mary, 'you will ... bear a son, and you shall call His name Jesus' (Luke 1:31). Angel ornaments can remind us of the angels that sang 'Glory to God in the highest!' (Luke 2:14) to the shepherds on that first Christmas night."

Sam was beginning to think that if Christmas was lost, it was lost only a little. "And what about the Christmas lights?"

"Christmas lights, hmmmm ..." Mother said. "What do you think, Sam?" she asked.

"Well," said Sam, "the tiny ones look like little stars."

"And who made the stars?"

"God did," Sam said proudly.

"You're right again!" Mother replied. "God **'made ... the stars'** (Genesis 1:16). In the Christmas story, who followed a special star to find Jesus?"

Sam knew right away. "The Wise Men!"

Mother smiled at him and pointed at something beneath the tree.

"Presents!" Sam shouted.

"The Wise Men followed the star for a long time. When they found Jesus, they gave Him **'gold and frankincense and myrrh'** (Matthew 2:11). These were presents for God's one and only Son," she explained.

"And what is the best present of all, Sam?" Mother asked. Sam knew the answer to this question.

"Jesus is the best present because He is for everyone," he said. Sam looked to the crèche on the mantel. Mary and Joseph and the shepherds were waiting for Sam to place the Baby Jesus in the manger on Christmas Eve.

When he thought about Jesus, Sam remembered a Bible verse he had learned in Sunday School, **"God is love"** (1 John 4:16).

"Sam," Mother said softly, "the invitation to your party at school had the word *holiday* on it. Do you know what that word means?"

He did not.

"It means *holy day.* Christmas is a holy day because it is Jesus' birthday."

Then Sam finally understood.

Merry Christmas was not lost after all. It was just hidden a little. And if *you* look, you can find it too.

Because Merry Christmas is everywhere!